If Picasso Went to the Zoo

By Eric Gibbons

And illustrated by

50 Art Teachers

If Picasso Went to the Zoo

An illustrated introduction to art history for children by art teachers

By Eric Gibbons
Illustrated by 50 art teachers

Cover editing by Dana Ranning
Copy Editing by Michelle Lovejoy & Paul Rybarczyk
Species Research by Christa Bellock
Publishing assistance by Dongkui Lin

Copyright 2015

ISBN-13: 978-1-940290-42-3
ISBN-10: 1940290422

Printer: Printed in Canada by Transcontinental Printing
Publisher: Firehouse Publishing: www.firehousepublications.com
Author Website: www.ArtEdGuru.com

 Thriving Animals, non-endangered

 Threatened/Vulnerable

 Endangered

 Critically Endangered

 Extinct

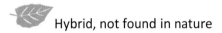 Hybrid, not found in nature

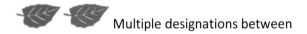 Multiple designations between

This book was conceived, written, and illustrated by 50 art teachers from all over the world who share a passion for art history and education. After the amazing success of Gibbons' first book, *If Picasso Had a Christmas Tree*, this follow-up book was created.

Each teacher has emulated an artist of his/her choosing from history and includes an alliterative animal in a way that honors the work of that artist. By combining art, history, science (zoology) and poetry, this book becomes a unique resource for inter-curricular teaching. A combination of art genres is used, from the Renaissance era to modern works, which may bear little resemblance to zoo animals! These art teachers, from elementary level to high school, created these delightful illustrations to share and educate. The contact information for every artist and the author is in the back of this book should you wish to purchase a print or an original work of art. Mr. Gibbons created the poems for each artwork.

We have also uploaded free multi-curricula lesson extensions you can print and share with students of all ages. These lesson extensions are found at www.artedguru.com/ifpicasso.html

Studies show that students who have art succeed at higher rates than their non-art peers. High school students in art outscore their peers by an average of 100 points on the SAT exam. Art makes connections to **all** curricula and promotes creative problem solving. Please support your local art department.

Art makes us smart!

If Pablo Picasso went to the zoo,
is this the kind of painting he'd do?
Polar bear ladies, Les Demoiselles,
I wonder what secrets they might just tell
of the artist Picasso, and his way of painting,
breaking down shapes, there is no mistaking
this style called cubism was what he created,
a new way of painting, at first it was hated,
people complained, "That's not how it looks!"
But Pablo now loved, his pictures fill books.

Eric Gibbons, *Pablo Picasso Polar Bears*, acrylic on canvas, 30 x 30 in.

If Giuseppe Arcimboldo went to the zoo,

is this the kind of painting he'd do?

Flowers and veggies fill up the space,

but hidden inside, can you see the face?

A rabbit in profile, an arctic hare,

living where cold and without a care.

Giuseppe was fond of painting for hours,

with fruits, and with veggies, and lots of flowers.

Can you draw a face and fill it with fruit?

Add in some plants and maybe a root.

Timothy Martin, *Giuseppe Arcimboldo Arctic Hare*, oil on canvas, 12 x 12 in.

If Hieronymus Bosch went to the zoo,
is this the kind of painting he'd do?
Surrealish barn owls do look rather wild,
and what is that thing they're sitting inside?
His work was unique, strange, and bizarre,
ahead of his time, really by far!
Paintings so dream-like were done by Dalí,
Bosch did them 500 years before he!
Some of his works are creepy and weird,
but the few that remain are deeply revered.

Rachel Wintemberg, *Hieronymus Bosch Barn Owls*, acrylic on canvas, 24 x 24 in.

If Roy Lichtenstein went to the zoo,
is this the kind of painting he'd do?
The leopard is perched up high in a tree,
kinda' cartoony, I think you will see.
Pop is the style of this artist's work,
it isn't by chance, or some kind of quirk.
Roy liked to use those dots called *benday*,
inspired by comics he read on Sunday.
To make his art graphic and make it stand out,
outlines and color is what it's about.

Amanda Miller, *Roy Lichtenstein Leopard*, multimedia, 12 x 12 in.

If Henri Matisse went to the zoo,

is this the kind of artwork he'd do?

Friend to Picasso or maybe a rival,

he was considered an artistic idol.

From painting, to sculpture, and paper collage,

his talents so awesome, it was no mirage.

Here a Macaw from paper that's blue,

with fanciful splashes of warm and cool hues.

When Henri was frail, unable to paint,

he'd cut up paper, 'cause quitter he aint!

Mary Jane Coker, *Henri Matisse Macaw*, painted paper cutout, 12 x 18 in.

If Ivan Albright went to the zoo,

is this the kind of painting he'd do?

This toothy reptilian is painting her face

with makeup and brush, she does it with grace.

A night on the town and meeting with friends,

I'm not very sure how this evening ends.

Ivan liked painting so dim and so moody

with people who lacked conventional beauty.

Textures so bold, contrasts so dark,

this gator's boyfriend might be a shark!

Chris Hodge, *Ivan Albright Alligator*, acrylic on canvas, 18 x 24 in.

If Robert Arneson went to the zoo,

is this the kind of sculpture he'd do?

Working with clay, ceramics he did,

often of faces, he played like a kid,

forming the clay in ways that were funny,

cartoonist by trade, and not for the money.

Aye-aye so silly, tongue and a wink,

this work is delightful! What do you think?

Can you make a face silly with clay?

If you haven't before, try it some day!

Yvonne Cavanagh, *Robert Arneson Aye-aye*, clay and glaze, 8 x 5 x 8 in. (Photo by Lisa Rudnick)

If Jean Michel Basquiat went to the zoo,

is this the kind of painting he'd do?

Jean was an artist from New York City,

born there and worked there, his work so gritty.

Pop was his style, graffiti he did,

on wall and on canvas, since he was a kid.

So buffalo, bison, are they the same?

Depends whom you ask, so what's in a name?

Basquiat painted with words and with symbol.

Can you do it too? It isn't so simple.

Gina Yacovelli, *Jean Michel Basquiat Buffalo*, acrylic on Arches paper, 12 x 12 in.

~~Buffalo~~
~~Bison~~
BuFFALo
Buffalo
......
1800 -
est 50 MILLION

1880's
> 1,000 ©

If Andy Warhol went to the zoo,
is this the kind of painting he'd do?
This graphic walrus is done up in purple,
printed and painted, all very commercial.
Pop artist Andy lived in New York,
making his special colorful work,
with brillo in boxes and many soup cans,
and paintings of so many Miss Marilyns.
Warhol was known from near and from far,
for more than 15, this man was a star.

Eric Gibbons, *Andy Warhol Walrus,* photocopy with oil pastel and digitally enhanced, 10 x 10 in.

If Jackson Pollock went to the zoo,
is this the kind of painting he'd do?
When he would paint he'd splash and he'd dribble,
all over the canvas and not just a little,
recording his actions as he would move,
almost like dancing to his kind of groove.
He didn't paint things, just splashed really big,
but if he'd paint a creature, it might be this pig.
Both may be messy, but this looks so sweet,
art does not always have to be neat.

Eric Gibbons, *Jackson Pollock Pig*, acrylic on canvas, 12 x 12 in.

If Lee Krasner went to the zoo,
is this the kind of painting she'd do?
Marred to Pollock, Jackson you know,
working together, he was her beau.
Koala is hiding up in a tree,
branches are framing him so you can see
this Australian cutie looking at us
in Krasner's loose style of *expressionust*.
Her paintings are bold with colors so bright,
fearless with hue, it just feels so right.

Leah Keller, *Lee Krasner Koala*, acrylic on canvas, 16 x 16 in.

If Elizabeth Catlett went to the zoo,
is this the kind of print she would do?
This woman of color born in the U.S.
studied in Mexico and learned to express
her feelings and thoughts all through her art,
portraits and printing expressing her heart.
Printers carve blocks with a sharp knife,
ink on its surface to bring art to life.
Here is a cougar in black and in white,
done in her style, does it give you a fright?

Lesli Wardell, *Elizabeth Catlett Cougar*, linoleum block print, 12 x 12 in.

If Salvador Dalí went to the zoo,

is this the kind of painting he'd do?

The clocks are all melting, it looks so absurd,

and look at that creature, a weird kind of bird.

Surreal was his style, as if in a dream,

a dodo bird here with time as a theme.

Dodos were friendly, too friendly I think,

for now they're all gone, completely extinct!

Eaten by sailors, and by their crew,

the last one was seen in 1662.

Holly Bess Kincaid, *Salvador Dalí Dodo*, acrylic on canvas, 10 x 10 in.

If Erté the artist went to the zoo,
is this the kind of painting he'd do?
An elephant draped in fabrics so fine,
covered in pattern and graphic outline.
Art Deco we say is the name of his style,
applied to this creature it does makes us smile.
I'll tell you a secret, you promise the same...
Erté you know is not really his name.
Romain de Tirtoff, a Russian born artist,
famous in Paris, some say the smartest.

Heather Lass, *Erté Elephant*, digital media, 14 x 14 in.

If El Greco, the Greek, went to the zoo,
is this the kind of painting he'd do?
Known by his nickname 'cause honestly, hey,
Doménikos Theotokópoulos was so hard to say!
He'd paint the angels, the saints, and the people,
with capes, and with staffs, and even a steeple.
This Renaissance artist painted it all,
and made them look slender and so very tall.
This giraffe is so lean, with blue stormy skies,
his work was unique, a feast for the eyes.

Sean Carney, *El Greco Giraffe*, acrylic on canvas, 12 x 12 in.

If Elizabeth Murray went to the zoo,

is this the kind of artwork she'd do?

Most artists like to paint on a square,

but Liz liked odd shapes that float in the air,

covered in colors so bright and so bold,

blue, purple, orange, and maybe some gold.

She often made pictures just made of lines,

shapes and some colors, all visual rhymes.

The monkey you see with banana so yellow,

looks like a happy and excited fellow.

Deborah Pey, *Elizabeth Murray Monkey*, acrylic on paper 14 x 14 in.

If Jessie Willcox Smith went to the zoo,
is this the kind of illustration she'd do?
Little Women, a book, that did bring her fame,
the pictures she made brought much acclaim.
Mother Goose was another series she painted,
if you don't know that one, please get acquainted.
Illustrators, you see, make pictures in books
to help readers see how everything looks.
This stork needs a story, help give it heart,
write a short tale, you just have to start.

Donna Cooper Smith, *Jessie Willcox Smith Stork*, watercolor and colored pencil on paper, 14 X 14 in.

If Alexander Calder went to the zoo,
is this the kind of sculpture he'd do?
Calder, an artist of many fine skills,
known from New York to Beverly Hills,
his father and grandpa were artists too,
but Alex did something so very new,
he invented the Mobile, art that could move,
his art had a motion, a new kind of groove.
His work was abstract, with color and shape,
can you see the camel, or is it an ape?

Hope Hunter Knight, *Alexander Calder Camel*, mixed media, 18 x 18 in.

If Helen Cordero went to the zoo,
is this the kind of figure she'd do?
Sculptor and potter of Cochiti Pueblo,
a Native American, wouldn't you know,
loved to make families made out of clay.
Here coatimundi gather and play.
Cousin to raccoons, they live in the trees,
eating up fruits, eggs, and some fleas.
Helen made sculptures of mother and child,
happy and playful, but never too wild.

Lorraine Pulvino Poling, *Helen Cordero Coatimundi*, ceramic with glaze, 9 x 4.5 x 5.5 in.

If Marcel Duchamp went to the zoo,

is this the kind of artwork he'd do?

This is a duck, it is not a joke,

please look again, your eyes are not broke.

You think it's a sponge hung on a string?

You're wrong, my dear reader, it is not that thing.

Dada's the name of this artist's style,

he liked to poke fun, it did make him smile.

He taught us that art needn't be serious,

it's fun to be silly, and maybe delirious.

Eric Gibbons, *Marcel Duchamp Duck,* Photograph, 10 x 10 in.

If Anne Truitt went to the zoo,
is this the kind of sculpture she'd do?
The style of her art was minimalism,
simple but powerful art symbolism.
Here a tarantula with eight skinny legs,
in colors of browns, greens, blacks, and reds,
these colors pair well with that giant spider.
I hope that it was not sitting beside her,
for some find them scary while others do not.
I like this spider, maybe a lot.

Eric Gibbons, *Anne Truitt Tarantula*, construction paper sculpture, 12 x 12 x 6 inches.

If Harriet Powers went to the zoo,
is this the kind of quilt she would do?
Born into slavery eighteen thirty-seven,
quilting, her art, was her kind of heaven.
This artist from Georgia led a hard life,
and art was a way to ease up her strife.
Here are some pelicans done in her style,
if you are like her, it will make you smile.
So when life is hard and makes you feel sad,
art breaks away from the hard and the bad.

K. Erica Dodge, *Harriet Powers Pelican*, quilted cloth, 21 x 21 in.

If Gustave Courbet went to the zoo,
is this the kind of painting he'd do?
This chimpanzee looks like he is stressed out,
endangered in nature is what it's about!
Courbet didn't like to paint what was pretty,
instead he made art to show us the gritty,
the pain, and the challenge of everyday life,
to struggle and work through our daily strife.
He turned his back on the art of romance,
realism, a style, the name of his stance.

Margaurita Spear, *Gustave Courbet Chimpanzee*, oil on panel, 14 x 14 in.

If Arthur Rackham went to the zoo,
is this the kind of art he would do?
This rhino does roam in a fantasy place,
a story unfolding in front of our face,
might there be witches or fairies around?
Be very quiet and don't make a sound.
Arthur was famous for the drawings he did,
for stories you've heard since you were a kid,
Alice in Wonderland, some by Shakespeare,
Illustrations we love and hold very dear.

Dawn Andre Beedell, *Arthur Rackham Rhinoceros,* ink, watercolor, graphite on paper, 12 x 12 in.

If Alma Thomas went to the zoo,

is this the kind of painting she'd do?

She was a teacher of art in a school,

but also a painter, isn't that cool?

The Whitehouse in DC likes her work too,

so her art is there for others to view.

She loved to paint dashes of colors you see,

and here is a toucan up in a tree.

Instead of whole bird, just part of its face,

staring at you or out into space.

Daryn P. Martin, *Alma Thomas Toucan*, acrylic on mat board, 17 x 17 in.

55

If Iris Nampeyo went to the zoo,

is this the kind of vessel she'd do?

Tewa her tribe, Hopi her home,

her people were forced to move and to roam.

Native American, land of her birth,

she made all her art from our mother earth.

Clay that was dug from ground with her hands,

turned into art and honor her lands.

Here, in her style, we see a small newt,

hardened in fire, and pulled from the soot.

Donald Peters, *Iris Nampeyo Newt*, ceramic 6 x 5 x 5in.

If Jan van Eyck went to the zoo,
is this the kind of painting he'd do?
Renaissance artist from Europe in Bruges,
here is his emu with turban in rouge.
Little survives of this artist's work,
except for his painting, he's dressed like a Turk,
with turban atop and fur coat below.
This artist's self-portrait is stunning you know.
It looks like this sample, except for a man,
an emu instead, 'cause with art you can.

Arlene Shelton, *Jan van Eyck Emu*, oil on canvas, 24 x 24 in.

If Alphonse Mucha went to the zoo,
is this the kind of illustration he'd do?
Art Nouveau was the name of his style,
sometimes on posters you'd see for a mile.
With edges like smoke, and bold flowing lines
that turn and twist like ornamentally vines.
Markhor with horns, made in his way,
is done in the French art nouveau way,
found in Iran and places nearby,
if you see a markhor, please do say hi.

Holly Bess Kincaid, *Alphonse Mucha Markhor*, watercolor, 12 x 12 in.

If M and C Escher went to the zoo,
is this the kind of illustration he'd do?
Patterns and drawings are things that he loved,
people, and creatures, and even a dove.
Maurits Cornelis was his real name,
math into art for him was a game.
Here an egret, a majestic bird,
eats fishes and frogs, or so I have heard.
Some are now threatened because of their plumes
to decorate hats, instead of some blooms.

Donna Staten, *MC Escher Egret*, pen and ink on paper with digital color, 12 x 12 in.

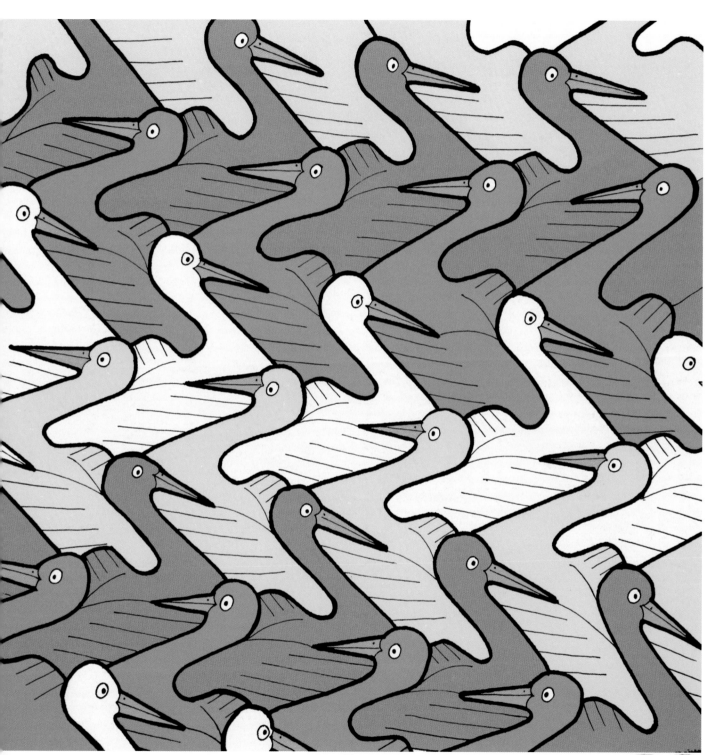

If Ms. Mary Blair went to the zoo,
is this the kind of painting she'd do?
Her name may be new but surely you know,
the work that she's done, it's been on a show,
like *Peter Pan* and another of Alice,
or Disney's "Small World," it looks like a palace.
In that small world, budgies we see,
sitting on windows or flying so free.
These birds from *down under*, called parakeets,
fly in great flocks in the Australian heat.

Cassie Stephens, *Mary Blair Budgies*, acrylic on paper with sculpey, 24 X 24 in.

If Rufino Tamayo went to the zoo,
is this the kind of painting he'd do?
This artist from Mexico, Oaxaca State,
loved painting watermelon, isn't that great!
This tiger agrees and grabs a big slice,
this modern art feline doesn't look nice!
Those teeth look so sharp, the valley so red,
I don't think I'd like to have that near my bed!
Surely intense, this painting has heart.
When paintings have feelings, we call it art.

Bárbara Martínez, *Tigre Rufino Tamayo*, mixed media on canvas, 14 x 14 in.

If Alice Baber went to the zoo,
is this the kind of painting she'd do?
This painter of expression liked making dots,
some in cool colors, some are in hots.
Most of her paintings are not of things,
just feelings she has, like when she sings.
But hidden inside this painting we see
a bison from Tucson roaming so free.
If you look closely you'll see him inside,
carefully gaze with eyes open wide.

Diane Stinebaugh, *Alice Baber Bison*, watercolor on paper, 18 x 18 in.

If Michelangelo da Caravaggio went to the zoo,
is this the kind of painting he'd do?
Known for his temper, reckless in life,
carried a sword and sometimes a knife.
His painting so gorgeous and dramatic too,
heavy with shadow and a dark hue.
His models were people he'd see every day,
but here capybaras painted his way,
ready to fight o'er a table of food,
maybe somebody said something too rude.

Amy Letts, *Caravaggio Capybaras*, acrylic on watercolor paper, 12 x 12 in.

If Niki de Saint Phalle went to the zoo,
is this the kind of sculpture she'd do?
Parisian girl in New York by three,
times were not easy so they had to flee.
Troubled in youth, art was her thing,
raising her spirits so they could take wing.
Paintings and sculptures bright in their color,
hers were so special, and not like another.
Covered in pattern, this sloth climbs a tree,
looks like it's fun, he's happy, you see.

If Marguerite Zorach went to the zoo,
is this the kind of painting she'd do?
Fauvists were artists called *wild beasts*,
they used crazy colors, a visual feast.
Here is a zonkey in blue and in yellow,
quite a unique and unusual fellow,
made when a donkey falls for a zebra,
is he a Pisces or maybe a Libra?
She was an artist for all of her years,
even Picasso was one of her peers.

Ian Sands, *Marguerite Zorach Zonkey*, acrylic on canvas, 18 x 24 in.

If Mr. George Segal went to the zoo,
is this the kind of sculpture he'd do?
He loved to use plaster to cover up things,
objects and people like these birdies' wings.
He rarely used color, leaving things white,
revealing the forms and reflecting the light.
Seagulls, you know, fly near the ocean,
this pair appears to be set in motion.
Maybe they're looking for shells on the shore,
or snack that's washed up from the sea floor.

Alycia Yates, *George Segal Seagulls*, mixed media, 23 x 18 in.

If N.C. Wyeth went to the zoo,
is this the kind of painting he'd do?
Two braves in the shadows creep without sound,
for deer, a white-tail, they've finally found.
Carefully stalking this six-pointed buck,
to feed both their families, it isn't just luck.
Hunting brought balance some time ago,
not killing for sport or showy ego.
Wyeth did pictures for many a book,
Deerslayer was one, do give them a look.

Trina Cole Harlow, *NC Wyeth White-Tail Deer*, watercolor on hot pressed cotton paper, 9 x 7 in.

If Rembrandt van Rijn went to the zoo,

is this the kind of painting he'd do?

Baroque is the name of the style he used,

painting in layers of light he diffused.

The drama was subtle, the shadows so bold,

making his paintings look very old.

Here is a hawk with a tail that is red,

looking at us as she turns her head.

What is she thinking, what does she see?

Maybe she'll soar in the sky and be free.

Ross Hines, *Rembrandt Red Tailed Hawk*, acrylic on canvas, 12 x 12 in.

If René Magritte went to the zoo,
is this the kind of painting he'd do?
This painting you see contains a small quote,
in French "This is not a mountain goat."
René did the same for a little brown pipe,
his silly fun way to make an art gripe,
complaining that art was becoming too stuffy,
he'd paint this goat, while making it fluffy.
Surreal was his style, but he added humor,
That often delighted the artful consumer.

Colin Temple, *René Magritte Mountain Goat*, acrylic on canvas, 14 x 18 in.

Ce n'est pas une chèvre de montagne

If Jean-Honoré Fragonard went to the zoo,
is this the kind of painting he'd do?
Rococo you know was the name of his style,
meant for the palace to make them all smile.
He painted for kings with subjects so rich,
some thought it vapid, superfluous kitsch!
Those are big words to call a flamingo,
maybe he's from good 'ol Santa Domingo.
Based on Jean's painting he titled *The Swing*,
looks like a fun day, early in spring.

Christa Bellock, *Jean-Honoré Fragonard Flamingo*, acrylic on canvas, 16 x 16 in.

If Beatrix Potter went to the zoo,
is this the kind of illustration she'd do?
Potoroo here meeting a friend,
to deliver a note that he had just penned.
Maybe a poem to a rabbit named Peter,
who moved to a home that is under a cedar.
Ms. Potter was famous for stories she wrote,
like *Peter the Rabbit* who did wear a coat.
She passed at the age of seventy-seven,
I'm sure she still draws way up in heaven.

Simone Lewis, *Beatrix Potter Potoroo*, watercolor and ink on board, 28 x 28 cm.

If Maria Martinez went to the zoo,
is this the kind of vessel she'd do?
Known for ceramics made from raw clay,
doing her work in the Pueblo style way.
From the south in the west, near Santa Fe,
she loved to make pottery every day.
Native American used lots of black,
some parts were shiny, some were left flat.
Here is a moth upon a small vase,
made oh so careful, with clay do not race.

Steve Wright, *Maria Martinez Moth*, ceramic, 8 x 10 in.

If Andrew Wyeth went to the zoo,
is this the kind of painting he'd do?
Son of N.C., Wyeth you know,
he loved to paint nature and loved to show
textures and people near where he lived,
his most famous a painting "Christina" he did.
He loved to paint wood, and beautiful textures,
creating a mood and catching the gestures.
These are wood ducks up in a tree,
with details so lovely for all us to see.

If Mr. Franz Marc went to the zoo,

is this the kind of painting he'd do?

This lover of animals used lots of blue,

maybe it was just his favorite hue.

Echoing curves and painted with passion,

these are all signs of his German expression.

The moose in this painting is done like he would,

captured with grace and just like he could.

Colors so brilliant, both warm and the cool,

Blaue Reiter in fact was the name of his school.

Dawn Eaton, *Franz Marc Moose*, acrylic on canvas, 12 x 12 in.

If Clementine Hunter went to the zoo,
is this the kind of painting she'd do?
She worked in the fields of the southern U.S.,
no school for this girl, I must confess,
but she learned to paint, and make her own art,
that opened a door, a new and fresh start.
She painted those fields, and the people she knew,
making them fun as she playfully drew.
This honey badger pulls a cart like a horse,
it's playful and joyful, like her art, of course!

Julie Kanya, *Clementine Hunter Honey Badger*, acrylic on paper, 14 x 14 in.

If Dorothea Tanning went to the zoo,
is this the kind of painting she'd do?
This tortoise is floating as if in a dream,
with doorways all open within this strange scene.
Painter and writer and sculptor and poet,
Dorothea artistic and gifted, we know it.
She married Max Ernst, to her he's the best,
together they moved to the desert Southwest,
away from New York, they made a great team,
with artists as spouses, life was a dream!

Kathy Carruba Schmidt, *Dorothea Tanning Tortoise*, acrylic on canvas, 9 x 9 in.

If Paul Cézanne went to the zoo,
is this the kind of painting he'd do?
This painter, a famous impressionist,
with work that inspired expressionists.
Brushwork so bold and color so warm,
helped give his paintings their unique form.
Cockatiel bird is perched on this table,
he'd eat all that fruit, if he were able,
See how this artist shaded with blue,
contrasting colors, reveal vivid hues.

Connie McClure, *Paul Cézanne Cockatiel,* oil on canvas, 10 x 10 in.

If Romare Bearden went to the zoo,
is this the kind of collage he would do?
He was a soldier in World War Two,
and studied in Paris where he learned to do
art that depicted American life,
for people of color, and of their strife.
Here a bald eagle, done like he might,
symbol of peace, and doing what's right.
Hand over hand, helping each other,
color ignored, just sister and brother.

Elizabeth Osborne, *Romare Bearden Bald Eagle*, magazine collage, 16 x 16 in.

If Theodor Geisel went to the zoo,

is this the kind of cartoon he would do?

Though not a real doctor, you know him as Seuss,

that is the name that he liked to use.

Forty-six books he wrote down and he drew,

maybe you know *Horton Hears a Who*.

Here a silk worm with a hat stops to say,

"Hello Mr. Moth, I wish you good day."

The clouds all whiz by and so does a bee,

in the style of Seuss, with a Seussian tree.

Gail Fountaine, *Theodor Seuss Geisel Silkworm*, acrylic on watercolor paper, 12 x 12 in.

If Mr. Paul Klee went to the zoo,
is this the kind of painting he'd do?
Paul liked to paint with a knife in his hand,
with colors and symbols, artwork so grand.
Here kookaburra with a face like he might,
painted with blade all through the night.
Layers of hue applied with rough shape,
yellow and orange, and even some grape.
Klee was connected to his inner kid,
nothing was fussy in art that he did.

Shari de Wever, *Paul Klee Kookaburra*, acrylic on canvas 17 x 17 in.

If Hyman Bloom went to the zoo,
is this the kind of painting he'd do?
A rabbi is what he wanted to be,
and the Russian empire he had to flee.
Often his art was filled with the pain,
from Aryan Nazis to old Pharaoh's reign.
Here by the water sits a baboon,
surrounded by colors and deep maroon.
Blue for the tears that were shed by the Jews,
red for their pain, in uncomfortable hues.

K. Lee Mock, *Hyman Bloom Baboon*, oil on panel, 24 x 24 in.

If Wassily Kandinsky went to the zoo,
is this the kind of painting he'd do?
This Russian born artist invented a style;
expressionism, it took him a while.
He painted his feelings with color and stroke,
all without subject, it wasn't a joke.
He thought that art should be what you feel,
not like a photo that held no appeal.
A kangaroo here is done like he might,
with colors and lines, I think it's done right.

Elena Klimova, *Wassily Kandinsky Kangaroo*, acrylic on canvas, 16 x 16 in.

If Friedensreich Hundertwasser went to the zoo,
is this the kind of painting he'd do?
Architect, artist, and also a Jew,
in difficult times during World War Two.
He hid from the Nazis by looking like them,
but also did art, his way to condemn
the terrible things we know that he'd seen.
Starting art school about age eighteen,
lover of colors he'd paint and he'd dab,
in hues and in patterns like this hermit crab.

Magi Chen, *Friedensreich Hundertwasser Hermit Crab*, mixed media, 35 x 35 cm.

If Georges Seurat went to the zoo,
is this the kind of painting he'd do?
The people of Paris stand by the Seine,
a river in France, so popular then.
Seals join the people to soak up the sun,
must be delightful, I bet it'd be fun.
George liked to paint with dashes and dots,
blue next to red and purple you've got.
Colors not mixed but painted nearby,
will magically blend within your mind's eye.

Connie McClure, *Georges Seurat Seals*, oil on canvas, 10 x 10 in.

If Georgia O'Keeffe went to the zoo,

is this the kind of painting she'd do?

This native New Yorker moved to the west,

out in the desert, she liked it the best.

She loved to paint flowers, bones, and the sky,

the mountains, the sands, and things that did fly.

Here is an Osprey, fish are their prey,

no fish in this desert, I don't think he'll stay.

It's pretty for sure with flowers and hills,

but he'll fly to water, soar for the thrills.

Sara Wisnewski-Olson, *Georgia O'Keeffe Osprey*, oil on board, 16 x 16 in.

If Fernand Léger went to the zoo,
is this the kind of painting he'd do?
He titled his style of working "Tubism"
but others just called it a kind of cubism.
He liked to paint patterns, and cylinder forms,
his art was unique, ignoring the norms.
Here is a llama that's painted his way,
looking at you as if it's to say,
"What do you think of my colorful pen?
I hope you come back to visit again!"

Emeralde Seaton, *Fernand Léger Llama*, acrylic on canvas, 12 x 12 in.

If Joan Miró went to the zoo,
could this be the kind of painting he'd do?
Sadly the mammoth is no longer here,
gone from this earth for many a year.
Hunted by men until they were gone,
now all we see are the ones that were drawn
upon the cave walls, way underground,
extinct long ago, they'll never be found.
This planet is fragile, we hope someone cares
for all of the creatures, and our future heirs.

Eric Gibbons, *Joan Miró Mammoth*, acrylic on canvas, 12 x 12 in.

If Pablo Picasso must leave the zoo,

is this the kind of painting he'd do?

A pangolin here in blue and cyan,

standing but hunched like a friendly old man.

This critter from Africa can roll in a ball,

so lions can't eat him, or hurt him at all.

He's really not blue, but painted that way,

'cause blue is a feeling when it's hard to say,

"Goodbye, my reader, we've come to the end,

this book is now over, we thank you, new friend!"

Eric Gibbons, *Pablo Picasso Pangolin*, oil on canvas, 30 x 30 in.

7: Eric Gibbons
Pablo Picasso Polar Bears
www.artedguru.com
www.firehousepublications.com

9: Timothy Martin
Giuseppe Arcimboldo Arctic Hare
www.timothymartin.com

11: Rachel Wintemberg
Hieronymus Bosch Barn Owls
thehelpfulartteacher@gmail.com
thehelpfulartteacher.blogspot.com

13: Amanda Miller
Roy Lichtenstein Leopard
Amillerk12@gmail.com

15: Mary Jane Coker
Henri Matisse Macaw
meejean@bellsouth.net

17: Chris Hodge
Ivan Albright Alligator
www.chodgeart.com
diebox1984-art@yahoo.com

19: Yvonne Cavanagh
Robert Arneson Aye-aye
www.yvonnecavanagh.com

21: Gina Yacovelli
Jean Michel Basquiat Buffalo
www.frandyjeangallery.com

23: Eric Gibbons
Andy Warhol Walrus
www.artedguru.com
www.firehousepublications.com

25: Eric Gibbons
Jackson Pollock Pig
www.artedguru.com
www.firehousepublications.com

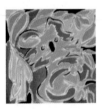

27: Leah Keller
Lee Krasner Koala
leeack080969@gmail.com

29: Lesli Wardell
Elizabeth Catlett Cougar
lesli.a.bachi@gmail.com

31: Holly Bess Kincaid
Salvador Dalí Dodo
capitolofcreativity.weebly.com

43: Lorraine Pulvino Poling
Helen Cordero Coatimundi
elseapea@yahoo.com

33: Heather Lass
Erté Elephant
lassartwork@gmail.com

45: Eric Gibbons
Marcel Duchamp Duck
www.artedguru.com
www.firehousepublications.com

35: Sean Carney
El Greco Giraffe
www.Carneystudios.net
www.Saatchiart.com/carney

47: Eric Gibbons
Anne Truitt Tarantula
www.artedguru.com
www.firehousepublications.com

37: Deborah Pey
Elizabeth Murray Monkey
debpey@aol.com

49: K. Erica Dodge
Harriet Powers Pelican
erica_ddg@yahoo.com

39: Donna Cooper Smith
Jessie Willcox Smith Stork
ddcsmith6157@gmail.com

51: Margaurita Spear
Gustave Courbet Chimpanzee
margauritaspear@gmail.com
margauritaspear.blogspot.com

41: Hope Hunter Knight
Alexander Calder Camel
Hopehknight@yahoo.com
www.dolvinartknight.blogspot.com

53: Dawn Andre Beedell
Arthur Rackham Rhinoceros
www.Dawnandrebeedell.com
dawnandrebeedell@hotmail.com

55: Daryn P. Martin
Alma Thomas Toucan
darynpmartin@gmail.com

67: Bárbara Martínez
Tigre Rufino Tamayo
babbiart@gmail.com

57: Donald Peters
Iris Nampeyo Newt
marashay@bellsouth.net

69: Diane Stinebaugh
Alice Baber Bison
dianeadams14@gmail.com

59: Arlene Shelton
Jan van Eyck Emu
arleneshelton@msn.com

71: Amy Letts
Caravaggio Capybaras
www.amuletts.com

61: Holly Bess Kincaid
Alphonse Mucha Markhor
capitolofcreativity.weebly.com

73: Kari Ann Jones
Niki de Saint Phalle Sloth
kariann1963@gmail.com

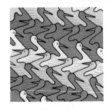

63: Donna Staten
MC Escher Egret,
donna.staten@sbcglobal.net
www.pinterest.com/artgirl90

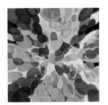

75: Ian Sands
Marguerite Zorach Zonkey
www.artofapex.com

65: Cassie Stephens
Mary Blair Budgies
cassiestephens.blogspot.com

77: Alycia Yates
George Segal Seagulls
alycia@alyciayates.com

79: Trina Cole Harlow
NC Wyeth White Tail Deer
Trinaharlow@yahoo.com
eARThshakingartteacher.blogspot.com

91: Michael Budden
Andrew Wyeth Wood Ducks
www.mikebudden.com

81: Ross Hines
Rembrandt Red Tailed Hawk
rosshines25@hotmail.com
www.hinesbrothers.com

93: Dawn Eaton
Franz Marc Moose
www.dawneaton.com

83: Colin Temple
René Magritte Mountain Goat
temple.elements@gmail.com

95: Julie Kanya
Clementine Hunter Honey Badger
Aerosmithgirl@sbcglobal.net

85: Christa Bellock
Jean-Honoré Fragonard Flamingo
Christabellock@gmail.com

97: Kathy Carruba Schmidt
Dorothea Tanning Tortoise
KathyCSchmidt@gmail.com

87: Simone Lewis
Beatrix Potter Potoroo
simonedlewis@gmail.com

99: Connie McClure
Paul Cézanne Cockatiel
connielmcclure@aol.com

89: Steve Wright
Maria Martinez Moth
wright271@sbcglobal.net

101: Elizabeth Osborne
Romare Bearden Bald Eagle
emd.osborne@gmail.com

103: Gail Fountaine
Theodor Seuss Geisel Silkworm
fontavd@aol.com

115: Sara Wisnewski-Olson
Georgia O'Keeffe Osprey
sara_wisnewski@hotmail.com

105: Shari de Wever
Paul Klee Kookaburra
sharidewever@gmail.com

117: Emeralde Seaton
Fernand Léger Llama
Emeraldearted@hotmail.com
eseatonarted@gmail.com

107: K.Lee Mock
Hyman Bloom Baboon
www.kleemock.com
k.leemock.art@gmail.com

119: Eric Gibbons
Joan Miró Mammoth
www.artedguru.com
www.firehousepublications.com

109: Elena Klimova
Wassily Kandinsky Kangaroo
elenaklim10@gmail.com

121: Eric Gibbons
Pablo Picasso Pangolin
www.artedguru.com
www.firehousepublications.com

111: Magi Chen
Hundertwasser Hermit Crab
chenmagi3@gmail.com

Discover more about animal conservation
with these respected organizations:

www.worldwildlife.org
www.nature.org
www.wcs.org

113: Connie McClure
Georges Seurat Seals
connielmcclure@aol.com

This book is dedicated to art teachers everywhere.

Art teachers know, when we grid, measure, and draw—we use geometry. When we make sculptures—we use engineering. When we mix colors—we reveal information about physics. When we create illustrations for stories—we learn about literature. When we review the styles of art from da Vinci to Bansky—we teach history. When we write about art—we strengthen these skills. When we create works of art, we solve complex visual problems in creative ways.

Evidence supports the fact that art students are more successful than their non-art involved peers by a significant margin. Students who take art succeed at higher rates than their peers on tests like the SAT, on average, by 100 points. The author's own students in 2013 scored 155 points higher than their peers, and were 50% more likely to pass the State assessment!

Please be an advocate for the arts in your own community.

See how it all started with our first book,
If Picasso Had a Christmas Tree

Many free lesson ideas and hand-outs at:
www.artedguru.com/ifpicasso.html

More great books and resources at www.FirehousePublications.com